Raintree is an imprint of Capstone Global Library Limited,
a company incorporated in England and Wales having its
registered office at 7 Pilgrim Street, London, EC4V 6LB –
Registered company number: 6695582

To contact Raintree:
Phone: 0845 6044371
Fax: +44 (0) 1865 312263
Email: myorders@raintreepublishers.co.uk
Outside the UK please telephone +44 1865 312262.

First published by © Picture Window Books in 2011
First published in the United Kingdom in paperback in 2014
The moral rights of the proprietor have been asserted.

Designer: Kay Fraser
Editor: Catherine Veitch
Originated by Capstone Global Library Ltd
Printed and bound in China

ISBN 978 1 4062 6619 1 (paperback)
18 17 16 15 14 13
10 9 8 7 6 5 4 3 2 1

British Library Cataloguing in Publication Data
A full catalogue record for this book is available from
the British Library.

Invisible Isabel

written by Adam and Charlotte Guillain
illustrated by Charlotte Cook

Isabel had lots of friends. But she often felt **invisible**.

Nobody seemed to notice her brand new rucksack.

Nobody seemed to notice her shiny new bike.

But **worst** of all, nobody seemed to notice
Isabel at home any more.
Ever since her little sister **Amy** had arrived,
Isabel had felt invisible.

But when Amy scribbled on the kitchen table,
Mum **did** notice Isabel.

"It's **your** fault for leaving the pens out,"
she said crossly.

And then Amy got to watch her favourite TV programme.
Nobody asked Isabel what she wanted to watch.

When Grandma came to visit, even **she** didn't seem to notice Isabel.

"What a clever girl Amy, you can say the word 'book'!" said Grandma.

"So what?" thought Isabel. "I can **read** books!"

Nobody noticed that Isabel could tie her own shoelaces.

Nobody noticed Isabel's great table manners.

They were only interested in Amy
– even when she was asleep!

"Am I completely invisible?" wondered Isabel.

"How can I get them to notice me again?"

"Perhaps I need to be more like Amy," thought Isabel as she wandered into the kitchen. And then she had an idea...

Grandma was the first to notice Isabel.

She was very surprised to find honey

all over the kitchen!

"Hey Grandma, look at me playing with honey!"
said Isabel. "Aren't I sweet, just like Amy?"

"Oh Isabel!" said Grandma. "I was just coming to tell you how **proud** of you I am. Amy is **lucky** to have such a wonderful big sister."

"Really?" asked Isabel.

"Yes!" said Grandma. "Amy hasn't stopped watching you all day!"

Isabel stopped to think.

Grandma was right – Amy noticed everything

her big sister did!

"Come on," said Grandma, 'let's clean up together.

Then I'd love you to read me a story!"

Isabel **smiled.**

She didn't feel invisible any more.

But she did feel a bit sticky!